Sleeping Nasty

Tony Bradman
Illustrated by Richard Watson

D1329093

White Wolves series consultant: Sue Ellis,
Centre for Literacy in Primary Education

This book can be used in the White Wolves Guided Reading
programme by more advanced readers in Year 2

www.acblack.com

Text copyright © 2009 Tony Bradman
Illustrations copyright © 2009 Richard Watson

ISBN 978-1-4081-2209-9

A CIP catalogue for this book is available from the British Library.

Chapter One

"Are you *sure* I have to do this?" said Prince Oscar, looking down at his parents. "I wish you would change your minds."

Oscar wasn't happy. He was sitting on his father's horse and wearing his father's armour. But Dobbin was a tired old nag, and the armour was rusty and dented.

"I'm afraid so," said the king, his face grim. "You know how bad things have been. This is our only chance to save ourselves."

"Your father is right," said the queen, her face even grimmer. "We're broke! If you don't succeed in this quest, we might end up living in a *tent*!"

The king and queen had run out of money. Now they had come up with a crazy plan. They were sending Oscar to find a rich princess – and *marry* her!

Oscar, however, didn't want to get
married. He was too young, and there was
lots of other stuff he wanted to do – to travel
the world … and see wonderful sights …

and meet interesting people.

"But… But…" Oscar spluttered, trying to think of a way to explain how he felt. It was too difficult, though. Besides, he was a good boy, and he wanted to help his parents.

"OK, then, I'll give it a whirl," he said. "But don't blame me if it all goes wrong."

Little did he know what lay ahead…

Chapter Two

Oscar and Dobbin set off down the road.
Day after day, they trudged through boring
villages and dull countryside.

Oscar searched everywhere, but he
couldn't find the right princess. Either they
were married, or they wouldn't talk to him.

Then, one sunny afternoon, he met an old shepherd.

"Oh, hi there," said Oscar, smiling. "Er … could you tell me if any rich princesses live around here? It's, well … quite important."

"Actually, there is *one*," said the shepherd, frowning. "Mind you, she's been fast asleep for nearly a hundred years…"

He told Oscar the strange story of Sleeping Beauty. Long ago, a daughter had been born to a king and queen. They had asked twelve fairies to bless the baby, but a bad fairy had turned up, too. She cursed the little princess, saying that one day she would prick her finger on a spinning wheel and die.

The other fairies couldn't remove the curse. But they *did* soften it, so the princess would just fall asleep until a prince came and woke her. Her parents banned spinning wheels from their kingdom, but it was no use.

Years later, the princess found an old spinning wheel in the attic of their castle – and pricked her finger on it. She fell into a deep sleep, and so did everybody else.

One hundred years later, the princess was still there, waiting for a prince to come…

"That sounds promising," said Oscar. "Where exactly is their castle?"

"First on the left, end of the lane," said the shepherd. "You can't miss it."

Oscar thanked him and rode off.

Chapter Three

"Whoa there, Dobbin!" said Oscar a few moments later.

The young prince looked up at the scary sight before him … and gulped.

The shepherd had been right. You couldn't miss the castle. But it was circled by a hedge of thorns – one so tall that only the very tops of the castle's highest towers could be seen poking up above.

"There doesn't seem to be a way in,"
said Oscar. "No wonder the princess is still
sleeping."

Dobbin neighed, but he didn't seem to
have any suggestions, so Oscar dismounted.

"Oh, well, here goes…"

Oscar walked up to the hedge, wincing
at the thought of struggling with those sharp
thorns. But he didn't have to – luckily, the
hedge parted and he walked through.

Inside the castle, it was very spooky. Everywhere Oscar looked, he found people who had fallen asleep in the middle of whatever they had been doing. And that's how they had stayed, enchanted for nearly one hundred years.

At last, Oscar went up some narrow stairs, and into the attic. A girl lay fast asleep beside a spinning wheel. She was snoring, and had a bit of dribble running from her mouth. But she was very beautiful.

"Er ... wakey, wakey!" said Oscar.

The girl didn't stir. Then he remembered how to break a magic spell. And kissed her.

The princess smiled and opened her big blue eyes… But her smile quickly vanished.

"Who are you?" she yelled. "And what took you so long?"

Chapter Four

"I beg your pardon?" said Oscar, who was quite shocked. The girl might be beautiful, but she was very bad tempered as well.

"Oh, never mind!" she snapped, jumping up and striding off down the stairs. "Come along, we'd better find Mother and Father and tell them the news!"

"Excuse me?" said Oscar, hurrying after her. "Er … what news is that?"

"Why, about our wedding, you stupid boy!" said the girl. "It's all part of the story. You wake me with a kiss, and then we get married. Although I have to say I was hoping for someone more handsome. And taller."

"Charming!" said Oscar, scowling.

The girl took no notice. Everyone in the castle had woken up by now. Most of them were just as grumpy as she was. There was lots of arguing and swearing, as things were dropped from stiff fingers and dozy people bumped into each other.

Oscar discovered that the girl was called Princess Prudence, although he had begun to think of her as Sleeping Nasty.

He also discovered that her parents were snooty and bad tempered, like her, and they didn't think much of him.

"He'll have to do, I suppose," said her mother, looking him up and down.

Oscar decided they were a nasty family. But he still had to marry the princess!

"*Psssst!*" someone hissed. "Quick, come over here, boy!"

Oscar turned round ... and saw a small woman with a wand waving at him!

Chapter Five

Oscar instantly realised that she was a fairy. She couldn't be anything else with her wings and her glittery black dress. She seemed to be hiding from the princess and her parents.

"Don't tell me," said Oscar. "You're the bad fairy, and you've come to put another curse on somebody. Well, go on then. Things couldn't be much worse."

"Sshh!" she hissed. "I *am* the bad fairy, or at least I was, once upon a time. But I don't want to make things worse for anybody. I feel guilty enough."

Oscar listened as she poured out her heart. Putting that curse on Princess Prudence had changed things for her, too. None of the other fairies would speak to her afterwards, and she had come to see the error of her ways.

Now she wanted to make up for what she had done, and *help* people instead of hurting them.

"That's great," said Oscar. "Actually, everyone seems to have woken up very bad tempered. Maybe you could put them back to sleep till they're a bit nicer."

"No problem!" said the fairy. "Is there anything you'd like yourself?"

"Oh, yes," said Oscar with a grin. "I have a couple of requests, actually…"

And so we come to the end of our story, and a very cheerful ending it is, too. The ex-bad fairy put everyone in the castle back to sleep, and added something to the spell that would make them nicer when they woke up.

Then she made Oscar's parents rich,
which meant that he could do what he liked.

So Oscar travelled the world … and saw
many wonderful sights … and met lots of
interesting people.

One day, he even met a beautiful
princess, who was also very sweet natured.
He could hardly believe his luck – so a week
later he asked her to marry him, and she
said yes, of course.

Which just goes to show – things never
turn out quite as you might think!